WHERE'S WALLY?

THE TOTALLY ESSENTIAL
TRAVEL
COLLECTION

MARTIN HANDFORD

WALKER BOOKS
AND SUBSIDIARIES
LONDON • BOSTON • SYDNEY • AUCKLAND

HI WALLY-WATCHER!

ARE YOU READY TO JOIN ME ON MY SEVEN
FANTASTIC ADVENTURES?

WHERE'S WALLY?
WHERE'S WALLY NOW?
WHERE'S WALLY? THE FANTASTIC JOURNEY
WHERE'S WALLY? IN HOLLYWOOD
WHERE'S WALLY? THE WONDER BOOK
WHERE'S WALLY? THE GREAT PICTURE HUNT
WHERE'S WALLY? THE INCREDIBLE PAPER CHASE

CAN YOU FIND THE FIVE INTREPID TRAVELLERS
AND THEIR PRECIOUS ITEMS IN EVERY SCENE?

ODLAW   WIZARD   WENDA   WOOF   WALLY
WHITEBEARD

 WALLY'S KEY   WOOF'S BONE   WENDA'S CAMERA

 WIZARD WHITEBEARD'S SCROLL   ODLAW'S BINOCULARS

WAIT, THERE'S MORE! AT THE BEGINNING AND
END OF EACH ADVENTURE, FIND A FOLD-OUT
CHECKLIST WITH HUNDREDS MORE THINGS
TO LOOK FOR.

WOW! WHAT A SEARCH!

BON VOYAGE!

Wally

WHERE'S WALLY?

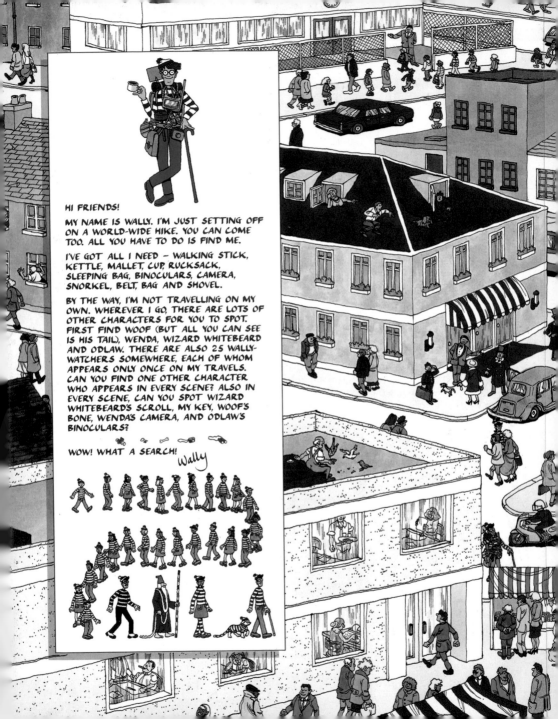

HI FRIENDS!

MY NAME IS WALLY. I'M JUST SETTING OFF ON A WORLD-WIDE HIKE. YOU CAN COME TOO. ALL YOU HAVE TO DO IS FIND ME.

I'VE GOT ALL I NEED – WALKING STICK, KETTLE, MALLET, CUP, RUCKSACK, SLEEPING BAG, BINOCULARS, CAMERA, SNORKEL, BELT, BAG AND SHOVEL.

BY THE WAY, I'M NOT TRAVELLING ON MY OWN. WHEREVER I GO, THERE ARE LOTS OF OTHER CHARACTERS FOR YOU TO SPOT. FIRST FIND WOOF (BUT ALL YOU CAN SEE IS HIS TAIL), WENDA, WIZARD WHITEBEARD AND ODLAW. THERE ARE ALSO 25 WALLY-WATCHERS SOMEWHERE, EACH OF WHOM APPEARS ONLY ONCE ON MY TRAVELS. CAN YOU FIND ONE OTHER CHARACTER WHO APPEARS IN EVERY SCENE? ALSO IN EVERY SCENE, CAN YOU SPOT WIZARD WHITEBEARD'S SCROLL, MY KEY, WOOF'S BONE, WENDA'S CAMERA, AND ODLAW'S BINOCULARS?

WOW! WHAT A SEARCH! Wally

GREETINGS,
WALLY FOLLOWERS!
WOW, THE BEACH WAS
GREAT TODAY! I SAW
THIS GIRL STICK AN
ICE-CREAM IN HER
BROTHER'S FACE, AND
THERE WAS A SAND-
CASTLE WITH A REAL
KNIGHT IN ARMOUR
INSIDE! FANTASTIC!

Wally

WHERE'S ON THE BEACH WALLY?

TO:
WALLY FOLLOWERS,
HERE, THERE,
EVERYWHERE.

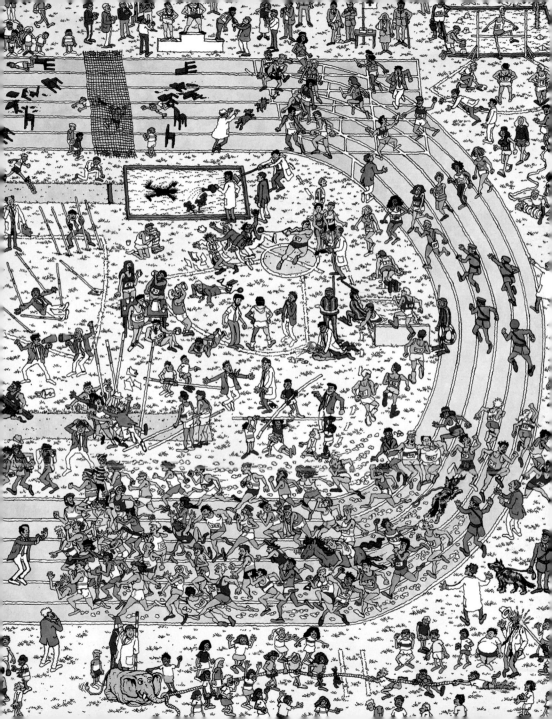

HOW-DE-DOO, WALLY SCHOLARS!
I'M CLEVER, AS YOU KNOW.
I GO TO MUSEUMS TO LEARN
THINGS. TODAY I FOUND OUT
ABOUT TICKLING THE TOES OF
A MAN IN THE STOCKS; ABOUT
KNOCKING DOWN A SUIT OF
ARMOUR; ABOUT THE
EGYPTIAN MUMMY'S BABY.
NOW THAT'S LEARNING!

Wally

TO:
WALLY SCHOLARS,
AT SCHOOL,
IN TROUBLE,
AGAIN.

ROLL UP, WALLY FUN LOVERS! WOW! I'VE LOST ALL MY THINGS, ONE IN EVERY PLACE. NOW YOU HAVE TO GO BACK AND FIND THEM. AND SOMEWHERE ONE OF THE WALLY-WATCHERS HAS LOST THE BOBBLE FROM HIS HAT. CAN YOU SPOT WHICH ONE, AND FIND THE MISSING BOBBLE?

Wally

TO:
WALLY FUN LOVERS,
BACK TO THE BEGINNING,
START AGAIN,
TERRIFIC.

WHERE'S FAIRGROUND WALLY?

THE ABSOLUTELY HUGE AND ENORMOUSLY INTERESTING BOOK OF CAVEMEN, CAVE WOMEN, CAVE DOGS AND ALL SORTS OF EXTREMELY SAVAGE STONE-AGE BEASTS.

HI THERE, BOOK WORMS!

SOME BITS OF HISTORY ARE AMAZING! I SIT HERE READING ALL THESE BOOKS ABOUT THE WORLD LONG AGO, AND IT'S LIKE RIDING A TIME MACHINE. WHY NOT TRY IT FOR YOURSELVES? JUST SEARCH EACH PICTURE AND FIND ME, WOOF (REMEMBER, ALL YOU CAN SEE IS HIS TAIL), WENDA, WIZARD WHITEBEARD AND ODLAW. THEN LOOK FOR MY KEY, WOOF'S BONE (IN THIS SCENE IT'S THE BONE THAT'S NEAREST TO HIS TAIL), WENDA'S CAMERA, WIZARD WHITEBEARD'S SCROLL AND ODLAW'S BINOCULARS.

THERE ARE ALSO 25 WALLY-WATCHERS, EACH OF WHOM APPEARS ONLY ONCE SOMEWHERE ON MY TRAVELS. AND ONE MORE THING! CAN YOU FIND ANOTHER CHARACTER, NOT SHOWN BELOW, WHO APPEARS ONCE IN EVERY PICTURE?

Wally

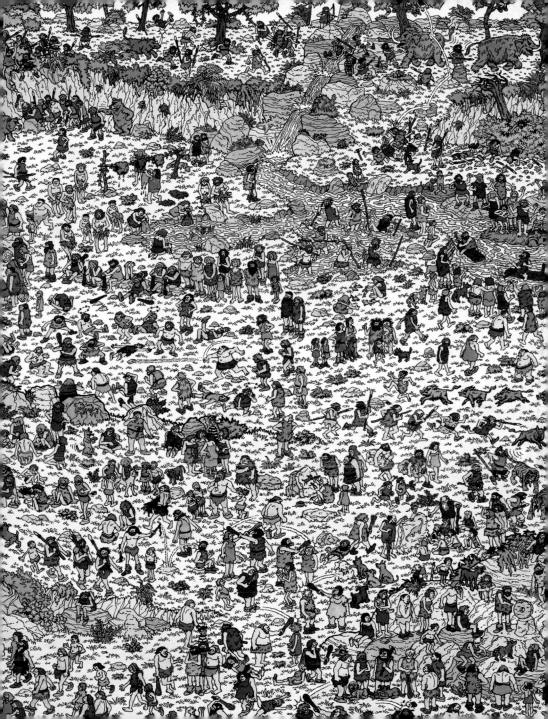

4,578 YEARS AGO

THE RIDDLE OF THE PYRAMIDS

THE ANCIENT EGYPTIANS WERE VERY CLEVER PEOPLE WHO LOVED GOATS, CATS AND SPHINX, AND INVENTED PYRAMIDS. WITH GREAT DIFFICULTY THEY BUILT SEVERAL HUGE PYRAMIDS IN THE DESERT.

BUT NOW NO ONE CAN REMEMBER WHY. WERE THEY ADVENTURE PLAYGROUNDS FOR EGYPTIAN MUMMIES AND BABIES, OR WERE THEY HOUSES WITHOUT ANY OF THE USEFUL BITS? IS IT POSSIBLE (OR EVEN LIKELY) THAT PHARAOHS WERE BURIED UNDER THEM? THESE QUESTIONS ARE AS HARD TO ANSWER AS A CAMEL'S HUMP.

2,000 YEARS AGO

FVN AND GAMES IN ANCIENT ROME

THE ROMANS SPENT MOST OF THEIR TIME FIGHTING, CONQVERING, LEARNING LATIN AND MAKING ROADS. WHEN THEY TOOK THEIR HOLIDAYS, THEY ALWAYS HAD GAMES AT THE COLISEVM (AN OLD SORT OF PLAYGROVND).

THEIR FAVOVRITE GAMES WERE FIGHTING, MORE FIGHTING, CHARIOT RACING, FIGHTING AND FEEDING CHRISTIANS TO LIONS. WHEN THE CROWD GAVE A GLADIATOR THE THVMBS DOWN, IT MEANT KILL YOVR OPPONENT. THVMBS VP MEANT LET HIM GO, TO FIGHT TO THE DEATH ANOTHER DAY.

1,003 YEARS AGO

ON TOUR
WITH THE
VIKINGS

At home the Vikings were quiet people, who liked knitting and cheese tasting and boring things like that. But on tour they went wild. They put on their best horned hats and sailed across the sea, singing and shouting like mad. If you heard them coming, it was best to run away, because once they had arrived and unpacked their axes, there was no holding them back.

The End of the Crusades

After 200 years of fierce argument with the Saladins and Paladins, who would not tell them the way to Jerusalem, the Crusaders finally ran out of clean tee-shirts, so they came home. For years afterwards they dined out on stories of the lovely castles they had battered and besieged and the fascinating people they had thrown rocks at, so the Crusades were not a complete waste of time after all.

ONCE UPON A SATURDAY MORNING

The Middle Ages were a very merry time to be alive, especially on Saturdays, as long as you didn't get caught. Short skirts and stripy tights were in fashion for men; everybody knew lots of jokes; there was widespread juggling and jousting and archery and jesting and fun. But if you got into trouble, the Middle Ages could be miserable. For the man in the stocks or the pillory or about to lose his head, Saturday morning was no laughing matter.

THE LAST DAYS OF THE AZTECS

The Aztecs lived in sunny Mexico and were rich and strong and liked swinging from poles pretending to be eagles. They also liked making human sacrifices to their gods, so it was best to agree with everything they said. The Spanish were also rich and strong, and some of them, called conquistadors, came to Mexico in 1519 to have an adventure. They thought the Aztecs were a complete nuisance, only good for arguing with and fighting.

400 YEARS AGO

Is red better than blue? What do you mean, your poem about cherry blossom is better than mine? Shall we have another cup of tea? Over difficult questions such as these, the Japanese fought fiercely for hundreds of years. The fiercest fighters of all were the samurai, who wore flags on their backs so that their mummies could find them. The fighters without flags were called ashigaru. They couldn't take a joke any better than the samurai, especially about their hair.

TROUBLE IN OLD JAPAN

250 YEARS AGO

BEING A PIRATE

(Shiver-me-timbers!)

It was really a lot of fun being a pirate, especially if you were very hairy and didn't have much in the way of brains. It also helped if you only had one leg, or one eye, or two noses, and had a pirate's hat with your name-tag sewn inside and a treasure-map and a rusty cutlass. Once there were lots of pirates, but they died out in the end because too many of them were men (which is not a good idea).

HAVING A BALL IN GAYE PAREE

The history of France has some very bad bits, like getting your head chopped off by Madame Guillotine in the French Revolution; and some very good bits, like the invention of smelly cheese. In 1870 Napoleon (the third one) threw a marvellous ball in Paris to celebrate 1870 being a good bit. All the beau- tiful people came and danced the night away to a band called the Third Republic.

100 YEARS AGO

THE GOLD RUSH

At the end of the 19th century large numbers of excited AMERICANS were fre- quently to be seen RUSHING headlong towards HOLES in the ground, hoping to find GOLD. Most of them never even found the holes in the ground. But at least they all had a GOOD DAY, with plenty of EXERCISE and FRESH AIR, which kept them HEALTHY. And health is much more valuable than GOLD . . . well, nearly more valuable . . . isn't it?

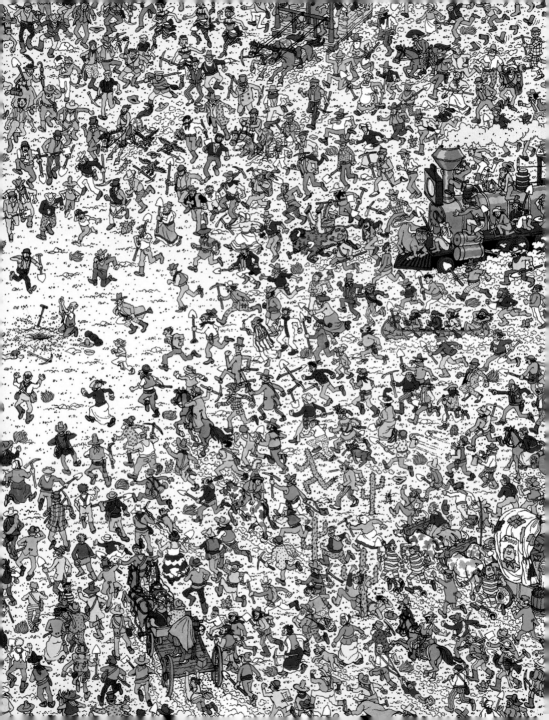

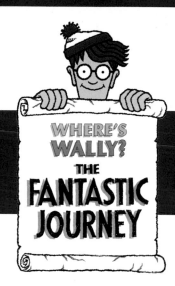

THE GOBBLING GLUTTONS

ONCE UPON A TIME WALLY
EMBARKED UPON A FANTASTIC
JOURNEY. FIRST, AMONG A
THRONG OF GOBBLING GLUTTONS,
HE MET WIZARD WHITEBEARD, WHO
COMMANDED HIM TO FIND A SCROLL AND
THEN TO FIND ANOTHER AT EVERY STAGE OF
HIS JOURNEY. FOR WHEN HE HAD FOUND
12 SCROLLS, HE WOULD UNDERSTAND THE
TRUTH ABOUT HIMSELF.

IN EVERY PICTURE FIND WALLY, WOOF (BUT ALL
YOU CAN SEE IS HIS TAIL), WENDA, WIZARD
WHITEBEARD, ODLAW AND THE SCROLL. THEN
FIND WALLY'S KEY, WOOF'S BONE (IN THIS SCENE
IT'S THE BONE THAT'S NEAREST TO HIS TAIL),
WENDA'S CAMERA AND ODLAW'S BINOCULARS.

THERE ARE ALSO 25 WALLY-WATCHERS, EACH OF
WHOM APPEARS ONLY ONCE SOMEWHERE IN
THE FOLLOWING 12 PICTURES. AND ONE MORE
THING! CAN YOU FIND ANOTHER CHARACTER,
NOT SHOWN BELOW, WHO APPEARS ONCE IN
EVERY PICTURE EXCEPT THE LAST?

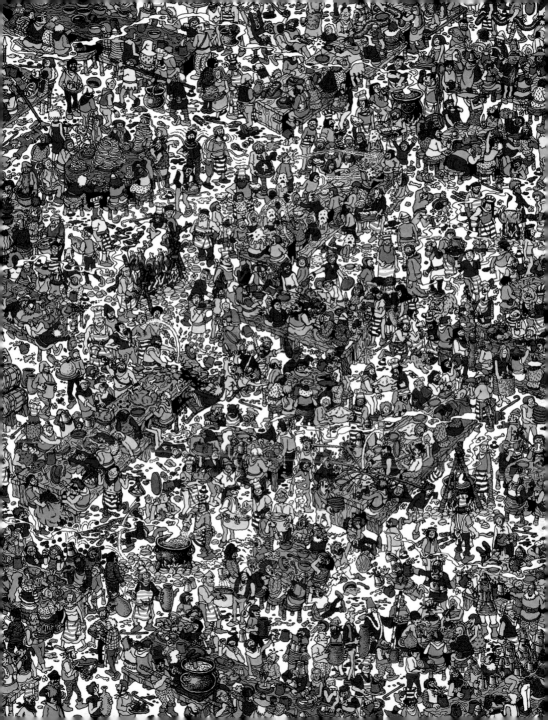

THE BATTLING MONKS

THEN WALLY AND WIZARD WHITEBEARD CAME
TO THE PLACE WHERE THE INVISIBLE MONKS
OF FIRE FOUGHT THE MONKS OF WATER. AND
AS WALLY SEARCHED FOR THE SECOND SCROLL,
HE SAW THAT MANY WALLIES HAD BEEN THIS WAY BEFORE.
AND WHEN HE FOUND THE SCROLL, IT WAS TIME TO
CONTINUE WITH HIS JOURNEY.

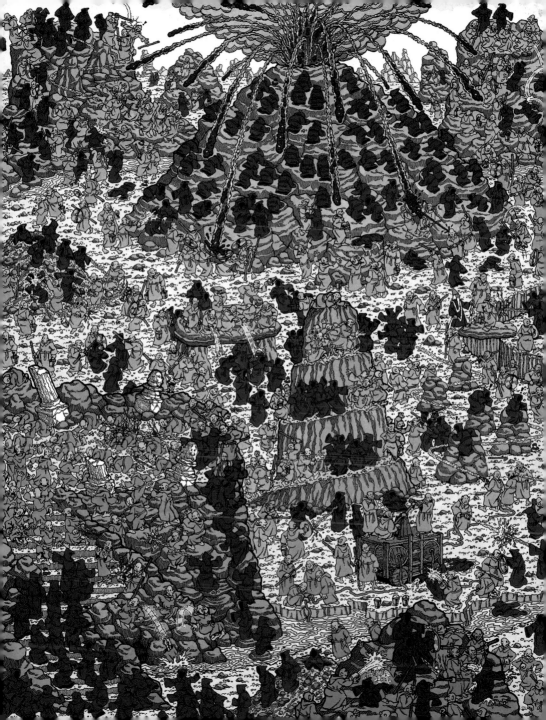

THE CARPET FLYERS

THEN WALLY AND WIZARD WHITEBEARD CAME
TO THE LAND OF THE CARPET FLYERS, WHERE
MANY WALLIES HAD BEEN BEFORE. AND
WALLY SAW THAT THERE WERE MANY
CARPETS IN THE SKY AND MANY RED BIRDS
(HOW MANY, OH BRAINY BIRD AND CARPET WATCHERS?).
AND WHEN WALLY FOUND THE THIRD SCROLL, IT WAS
TIME TO CONTINUE WITH HIS JOURNEY.

THE GREAT BALL-GAME PLAYERS

THEN WALLY AND WIZARD WHITEBEARD CAME TO
THE PLAYING FIELD OF THE GREAT BALL-GAME
PLAYERS, WHERE MANY WALLIES HAD BEEN BEFORE.
AND WALLY SAW THAT FOUR TEAMS WERE PLAYING AGAINST
EACH OTHER (BUT WAS ANYONE WINNING? WHAT WAS THE
SCORE? CAN YOU WORK OUT THE RULES?). THEN WALLY FOUND
THE FOURTH SCROLL AND CONTINUED WITH HIS JOURNEY.

THE FEROCIOUS RED DWARVES

THEN WALLY AND WIZARD WHITEBEARD CAME
AMONG THE FEROCIOUS RED DWARVES, WHERE
MANY WALLIES HAD BEEN BEFORE. AND THE
DWARVES WERE ATTACKING THE MANY-COLOURED
SPEARMEN, CAUSING MIGHTY MAYHEM AND HORRID
HAVOC. AND WALLY FOUND THE FIFTH SCROLL, AND
CONTINUED WITH HIS JOURNEY.

THE NASTY NASTIES

THEN WALLY AND WIZARD WHITEBEARD CAME TO
THE CASTLE OF THE NASTY NASTIES, WHERE
MANY WALLIES HAD BEEN BEFORE. AND
WHEREVER WALLY WALKED, THERE WAS A CLATTERING
OF BONES (WOOF'S BONE IN THIS SCENE IS THE NEAREST TO
HIS TAIL) AND A FOUL SLURPING OF FILTHY FOOD. AND WALLY
FOUND THE SIXTH SCROLL AND CONTINUED WITH HIS JOURNEY.

THE FIGHTING FORESTERS

THEN WALLY AND WIZARD WHITEBEARD CAME
AMONG THE FIGHTING FORESTERS, WHERE
MANY WALLIES HAD BEEN BEFORE. AND IN THEIR
BATTLE WITH THE EVIL BLACK KNIGHTS, THE
FOREST WOMEN WERE AIDED BY THE ANIMALS, BY THE LIVING
MUD, EVEN BY THE TREES THEMSELVES. AND WALLY FOUND THE
SEVENTH SCROLL AND CONTINUED WITH HIS JOURNEY.

THE DEEP-SEA DIVERS

THEN WALLY AND WIZARD WHITEBEARD CAME TO
THE WATERY WORLD OF THE DEEP-SEA DIVERS,
WHERE MANY WALLIES HAD BEEN BEFORE. AND
WALLY SEARCHED FOR THE EIGHTH SCROLL AMONG
THE MONSTERS OF THE DEEP, AMONG THE MERMAIDS,
FISHERMEN AND FISH. AND WHEN HE FOUND IT, IT WAS TIME
TO CONTINUE WITH HIS JOURNEY.

THE KNIGHTS OF THE MAGIC FLAG

THEN WALLY AND WIZARD WHITEBEARD CAME
TO A PLACE MORE CROWDED THAN ANY WALLY
HAD SEEN BEFORE, WHERE TWO ARMIES WITH
MANY MAGIC FLAGS WERE LOCKED IN COMBAT.
AND WALLY SAW THAT MANY WALLIES HAD BEEN THIS WAY
BEFORE. AND WHEN HE FOUND THE NINTH SCROLL, IT WAS
TIME TO CONTINUE WITH HIS JOURNEY.

THE UNFRIENDLY GIANTS

THEN WALLY AND WIZARD WHITEBEARD CAME TO
THE LAND OF THE UNFRIENDLY GIANTS, WHERE
MANY WALLIES HAD BEEN BEFORE. AND WALLY
SAW THAT THE GIANTS WERE HORRIDLY
HARASSING THE LITTLE PEOPLE. AND WHEN HE FOUND THE
TENTH SCROLL, IT WAS TIME TO CONTINUE WITH HIS JOURNEY.

THE UNDERGROUND HUNTERS

THEN WALLY AND WIZARD WHITEBEARD CAME
AMONG THE UNDERGROUND HUNTERS, WHERE
MANY WALLIES HAD BEEN BEFORE. AND THERE
WAS MUCH MENACE IN THIS PLACE, AND A
MULTITUDE OF MALEVOLENT MONSTERS. AND
WALLY FOUND THE ELEVENTH SCROLL AND CONTINUED
WITH HIS JOURNEY.

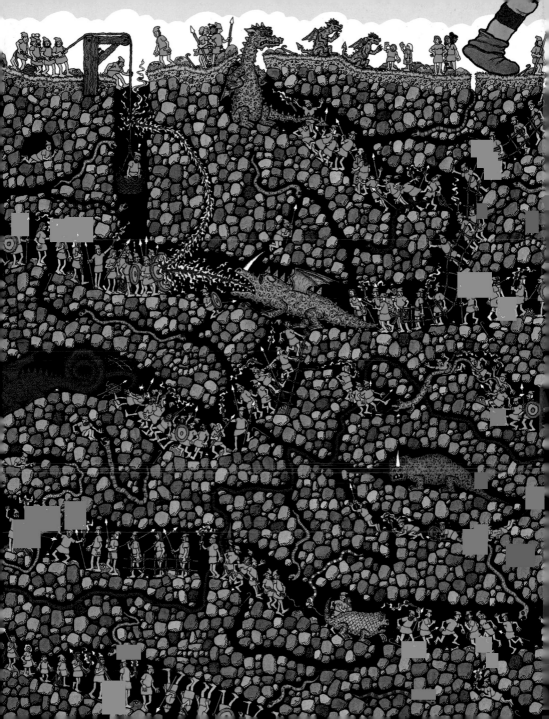

THE LAND OF WALLIES

THEN WALLY FOUND THE TWELFTH SCROLL AND SAW THE TRUTH ABOUT HIMSELF, THAT HE WAS JUST ONE WALLY AMONG MANY. HE SAW TOO THAT WALLIES OFTEN LOSE THINGS, FOR HE HIMSELF HAD LOST ONE SHOE. AND AS HE LOOKED FOR HIS SHOE, HE DISCOVERED THAT WIZARD WHITEBEARD WAS NOT HIS ONLY FELLOW TRAVELLER. THERE WERE NOW ELEVEN OTHERS – ONE FROM EVERY PLACE HE HAD BEEN TO – WHO HAD JOINED HIM ONE BY ONE ALONG THE WAY. SO NOW (OH LOYAL FOLLOWERS OF WALLY!) FIND THE REAL WALLY AND HELP HIM FIND HIS MISSING SHOE. AND THERE, IN THE LAND OF WALLIES, MAY WALLY LIVE HAPPILY EVER AFTER.

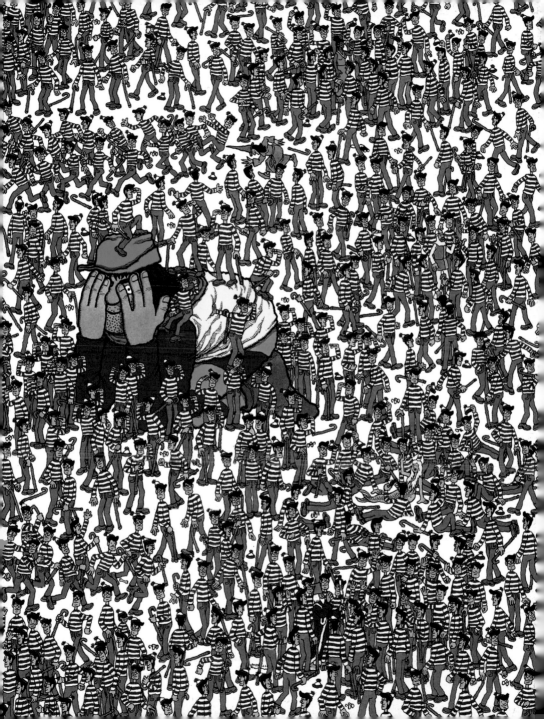

A DREAM COME TRUE

WOW, WALLY-WATCHERS, THIS IS FANTASTIC, I'M REALLY IN HOLLYWOOD! LOOK AT THE FILM PEOPLE EVERYWHERE – I WONDER WHAT MOVIES THEY'RE MAKING. THIS IS MY DREAM COME TRUE ... TO MEET THE DIRECTORS AND ACTORS, TO WALK THROUGH THE CROWDS OF EXTRAS, TO SEE BEHIND THE SCENES! PHEW, I WONDER IF I'LL APPEAR IN A MOVIE MYSELF!

★ ★ ★ WHAT TO LOOK FOR IN HOLLYWOOD! ★ ★ ★

WELCOME TO TINSELTOWN, WALLY-WATCHERS! THESE ARE THE PEOPLE AND THINGS TO LOOK FOR AS YOU WALK THROUGH THE FILM SETS WITH WALLY.

★ FIRST (OF COURSE!) WHERE'S WALLY?

★ NEXT FIND WALLY'S CANINE COMPANION, WOOF – REMEMBER, ALL YOU CAN SEE IS HIS TAIL!

★ THEN FIND WALLY'S FRIEND, WENDA!

★ ABRACADABRA! NOW FOCUS IN ON WIZARD WHITEBEARD!

★ BOO! HISS! HERE COMES THE BAD GUY, ODLAW!

★ NOW SPOT THESE 25 WALLY-WATCHERS, EACH OF WHOM APPEARS ONLY ONCE BEFORE THE FINAL FANTASTIC SCENE!

★ WOW! INCREDIBLE! SPOT ONE OTHER CHARACTER WHO APPEARS IN EVERY SCENE EXCEPT THE LAST!

★ ★ KEEP ON SEARCHING! THERE'S MORE TO FIND! ★ ★

ON EVERY SET FIND WALLY'S LOST KEY!

WOOF'S LOST BONE! WENDA'S LOST CAMERA! WIZARD WHITEBEARD'S SCROLL! ODLAW'S LOST BINOCULARS! AND A MISSING CAN OF FILM!

★ ★ ★ ★ AND MORE AND MORE! ★ ★ ★

EACH OF THE FOUR POSTERS ON THE WALL OVER THERE IS PART OF ONE OF THE FILM SETS WALLY IS ABOUT TO VISIT. ★ FIND OUT WHERE THE POSTERS CAME FROM. ★ THEN SPOT ANY DIFFERENCES BETWEEN THE POSTERS AND THE SETS.

SHHH! THIS IS A SILENT MOVIE

SO THIS IS HOW THE HOLLYWOOD DREAM BEGAN — WITH SILENT MOVIES MADE IN BLACK AND WHITE. IT LOOKS CRAZY AND IT MAKES YOU LAUGH. ACTING IN SLAPSTICK COMEDIES MUST BE REALLY HARD — LOOK HOW MANY ACCIDENTS ARE HAPPENING. BUT THE GREAT THING IS THAT NONE OF THE ACTORS EVER GET HURT, HOWEVER OFTEN THEY FALL FLAT ON THEIR FACES!

HORSEPLAY IN TROY

WHAT A SPECTACULAR SCENE THIS IS, WALLY-WATCHERS! AND WHAT AN EPIC COMMOTION PICTURE! I WONDER WHY THE TROJANS DIDN'T GUESS THE WOODEN HORSE WAS FULL OF GREEKS, AND HOW DID THEY GET IT THROUGH THE GATES OF TROY ANYWAY? I WOULDN'T LIKE TO BE IN THE TROJANS' SANDALS, IF THE COSTUME DEPARTMENT HAD GIVEN THEM ANY, THAT IS!

FUN IN THE FOREIGN LEGION

PHEW, FILM FANS, DON'T GET OVERHEATED, THIS IS THE MOST SIZZLING LOCATION SO FAR! EVERYONE'S SWELTERING, FROM STARS TO SAND-SHIFTERS. SOME OF THOSE EXTRAS LOOK LIKE THEY'RE LOSING THEIR COOL – HAVE THEY FORGOTTEN THIS IS ONLY A FILM? PERHAPS IT'S TIME A FEW MORE OF THEM DESERTED THE DESERT AND JOINED THE RUSH FOR ICE-CREAM!

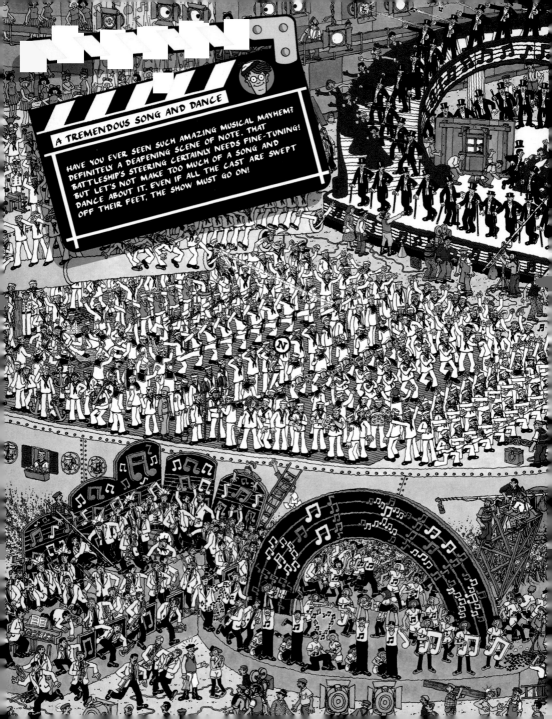

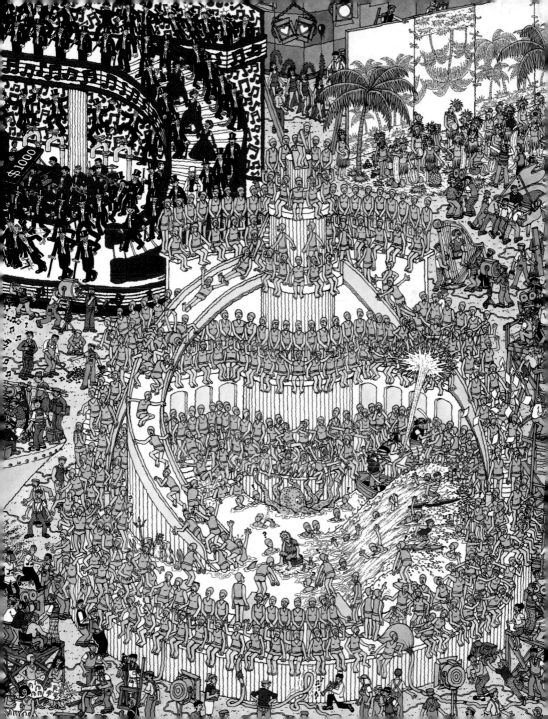

ALI BABA AND THE FORTY THIEVES

WHAT A CRUSH IN THE CAVE, WALLY-FOLLOWERS, BUT
PAN IN ON THOSE POTS OF TREASURE! HOW MANY
THIEVES WERE IN THE STORY? I BELIEVE THIS DIRECTOR
THINKS FORTY THOUSAND! HAVE YOU SPOTTED ALI BABA?
HE'S IN THE ALLEY, CUTTING HAIR – THE SCRIPTWRITER
THINKS HIS NAME'S ALLEY BARBER! JANGLING GENIES –
WHAT A FEARFULLY FUNNY FLICK THIS IS!

THE WILD, WILD WEST

YEEE-HA, WALLY-WATCHERS, HAVE YOU EVER SEEN SUCH A WILD, WILD WESTERN? HERE COMES THE WAGON TRAIN, STEAMING INTO TOWN; THE GOLD RUSH IS ON AND A COWBOY IS RIDING OFF INTO THE SUNSET! THERE'S SO MUCH ACTION, SO MUCH EXCITEMENT! I WONDER IF THE REAL WILD WEST WAS AS BRIGHT AND COLOURFUL AS THIS!

THE SWASHBUCKLING MUSKETEERS

ALL FOR ONE, ONE FOR ALL! – WASN'T THAT THE MOTTO OF THE THREE MUSKETEERS? NOW LOOK AT THIS FREE-FOR-ALL! CAN YOU SPOT OUR THREE GALLANT HEROES BATTLING WITH THE RED-COATED CARDINAL'S GUARDS? WITH ALL THIS SWASHBUCKLING ACTION GOING ON, I WONDER HOW THE CAMERAMEN CAN CAPTURE IT ALL ON FILM!

DINOSAURS, SPACEMEN AND GHOULS

PHEW, INCREDIBLE! TIME, SPACE AND HORROR ARE IN A MIGHTY MUDDLE HERE! WHAT COSMIC COSTUMES AND WHAT GREAT SPECIAL EFFECTS! ONE OF THOSE FLYING SAUCERS LOOKS LIKE IT'S REALLY FLYING! ARE THOSE REAL ALIENS INSIDE, NOT ACTORS AT ALL? SO WHAT'S REAL AND WHAT'S MADE UP IN FILMS LIKE THESE?

ROBIN HOOD'S MERRY MESS-UP

LOOK HOW MANY MERRY MEN HAVE LEFT SHERWOOD FOREST FOR A DAY OUT IN NOTTINGHAM CASTLE! AND WHAT A MERRY TIME THEY'RE HAVING, MESSING UP THE SHERIFF'S PARADE. WHICH ONE IS ROBIN HOOD? THE ONE WEARING A ROBIN HOOD, OF COURSE! WHEN YOU GO TO SEE THIS FILM, YOU'LL THINK IT'S ALL REAL, BUT THE CASTLE'S STONE WALLS ARE MADE OF WOOD!

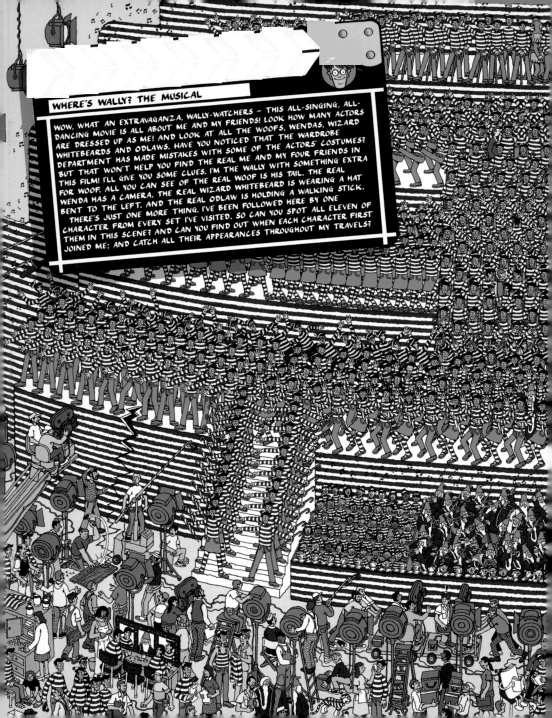

WHERE'S WALLY? THE MUSICAL

WOW, WHAT AN EXTRAVAGANZA, WALLY-WATCHERS – THIS ALL-SINGING, ALL-DANCING MOVIE IS ALL ABOUT ME AND MY FRIENDS! LOOK HOW MANY ACTORS ARE DRESSED UP AS ME! AND LOOK AT ALL THE WOOFS, WENDAS, WIZARD WHITEBEARDS AND ODLAWS. HAVE YOU NOTICED THAT THE WARDROBE DEPARTMENT HAS MADE MISTAKES WITH SOME OF THE ACTORS' COSTUMES? BUT THAT WON'T HELP YOU FIND THE REAL ME AND MY FOUR FRIENDS IN THIS FILM! I'LL GIVE YOU SOME CLUES. I'M THE WALLY WITH SOMETHING EXTRA FOR WOOF. ALL YOU CAN SEE OF THE REAL WOOF IS HIS TAIL. THE REAL WENDA HAS A CAMERA. THE REAL WIZARD WHITEBEARD IS WEARING A HAT BENT TO THE LEFT. AND THE REAL ODLAW IS HOLDING A WALKING STICK.

THERE'S JUST ONE MORE THING. I'VE BEEN FOLLOWED HERE BY ONE CHARACTER FROM EVERY SET I'VE VISITED. SO CAN YOU SPOT ALL ELEVEN OF THEM IN THIS SCENE? AND CAN YOU FIND OUT WHEN EACH CHARACTER FIRST JOINED ME; AND CATCH ALL THEIR APPEARANCES THROUGHOUT MY TRAVELS?

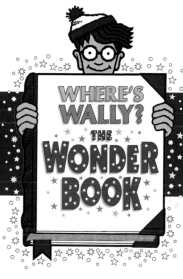

Once Upon A Page

HEY, WALLY FANS! LOOK AT ALL THESE BRILLIANT BOOKS! LOOK AT ALL THE CHARACTERS WHO HAVE STEPPED OUT FROM THEIR PAGES! WOW! WHAT A MAGIC SCENE! THESE BOOKS HAVE REALLY COME ALIVE! FANTASTIC – THAT BOOK OVER THERE IS ABOUT MY TRAVELS! AND WOOF, WENDA, WIZARD WHITEBEARD AND ODLAW ALL HAVE SPECIAL BOOKS OF THEIR OWN. NOW YOU CAN JOIN US TOO, IF YOU CAN FIND US, AND WE'LL TRAVEL TOGETHER THROUGH ALL THE OTHER WONDERFUL SCENES IN THIS WONDER BOOK. ONE SCENE IS MY SPECIAL FAVOURITE – YOU'LL NEVER GUESS WHAT MAKES IT SO GREAT. THE BOOKMARK MARKS IT, SO WHEN WE GET THERE, YOU WILL KNOW. NOW GET SEARCHING, WALLY FOLLOWERS, AND OFF WE GO! AND BE PREPARED FOR LOTS OF SURPRISES ALONG THE WAY!

Wally

THE SEARCH IS ON! FIND THESE FIVE INTREPID TRAVELLERS IN EVERY SCENE IN THE WONDER BOOK!

- FIND WALLY ... WHO TRAVELS EVERYWHERE!
- FIND WOOF ... WHO WAGS HIS TAIL! (WHICH IS ALL YOU CAN SEE!)
- FIND WENDA ... WHO TAKES THE PICTURES!
- FIND WIZARD WHITEBEARD ... WHO CASTS THE SPELLS!
- FIND ODLAW ... WHOSE GOOD DEEDS ARE FEW INDEED!

THE SEARCH CONTINUES! NEXT FIND THESE IMPORTANT THINGS THE TRAVELLERS HAVE LOST!

- FIND WALLY'S LOST KEY!
- FIND WOOF'S LOST BONE!
- FIND WENDA'S LOST CAMERA!
- FIND WIZARD WHITEBEARD'S MAGIC SCROLL!
- FIND ODLAW'S LOST BINOCULARS!

THE GREAT BOOK OF ODLAW'S GOOD DEEDS

CLASSIC STORIES FROM LITERATURE

BOOK OF SERY MES

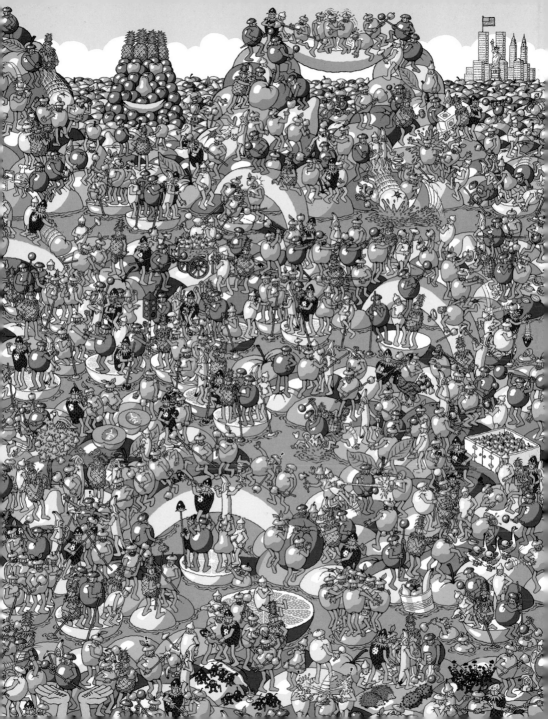

THE GAME OF GAMES

STARTED! CAN YOU SPOT THE ONLY ORANGE TEAM PLAYER WHO HAS FINISHED? AND THE ONLY GREEN TEAM PLAYER WHO HAS NOT YET BEGUN?

FOUR HUGE TEAMS ARE PLAYING THIS GREAT GAME OF GAMES. THE REFEREES ARE TRYING TO SEE THAT NO ONE BREAKS THE RULES. BETWEEN THE STARTING-LINE AT THE TOP AND THE FINISHING-LINE AT THE BOTTOM, THERE ARE LOTS OF PUZZLES, BOOBY-TRAPS AND TESTS. THE GREEN TEAMS NEARLY WON, AND THE ORANGE TEAM'S HARDLY

TOYS!
TOYS!
TOYS!

WOW! ALL THE TEENY-TINY TOY CREATURES ARE COMING OUT OF THE TOYBOX TO EXPLORE THE PLAYROOM! THE BOOKS ARE TOO HUGE TO READ, BUT THE GREEN ONE IS PERFECT AS A FOOTBALL PITCH! SWOOSH! AND THE BOOKMARK MAKES A BRILLIANT SLIDE! CAN YOU SEE A TEDDY TAKING OFF IN A PAPER PLANE? AND A DINOSAUR CHASING A CAVEMAN? WHAT HIGH JINKS AND HIGHWIRE ACTS ARE HAPPENING HERE! SO DO YOU THINK THAT THE TOYS ALWAYS HAVE GREAT TIMES LIKE THESE WHEN NO ONE IS ABOUT?

BRIGHT LIGHTS AND NIGHT FRIGHTS

HEY! WHAT BLAZING BEAMS OF LIGHT, WHAT A DAZZLING DISPLAY! GLITTER, TWINKLE, SPARKLE, FLASH – LOOK HOW BRIGHTLY THESE LIGHTHOUSES LIGHT UP THE NIGHT! BUT OH NO, THE MONSTERS WANT TO PUT THE LIGHTS OUT! THEY'RE ATTACKING FROM ALL SIDES. THE SAILORS ARE SQUIRTING PINK GUNGE AT THEM, BUT THE MONSTERS SPURT GREEN GUNGE RIGHT BACK! BUT WAIT! THREE OF THE MONSTERS ARE FIRING DIFFERENT COLOURED GUNGE! SPLASH, SPLAT, SPLURGE! CAN YOU SEE THEM, WALLY-WATCHERS?

THE CAKE FACTORY

MMMM! FEAST YOUR EYES, WALLY-WATCHERS! SNIFF THE DELICIOUS SMELLS OF BAKING CAKES! DROOL AT THE TASTY TOPPINGS! CAN YOU SEE A CAKE LIKE A TEAPOT, A CAKE LIKE A HOUSE, A CAKE SO TALL A WORKER ON THE FLOOR ABOVE IS LICKING IT? CAKES, CAKES, EVERYWHERE! HOW SCRUMPTIOUS! HOW YUM-YUM-YUMPTIOUS! LOOK

AT THE OOZING SUGAR ICING AND THE SHINY RED CHERRIES ON THE ROOF UP THERE! THAT ROOM IS WHERE THE FACTORY CONTROLLERS WORK, BUT HAVE THEY LOST CONTROL?

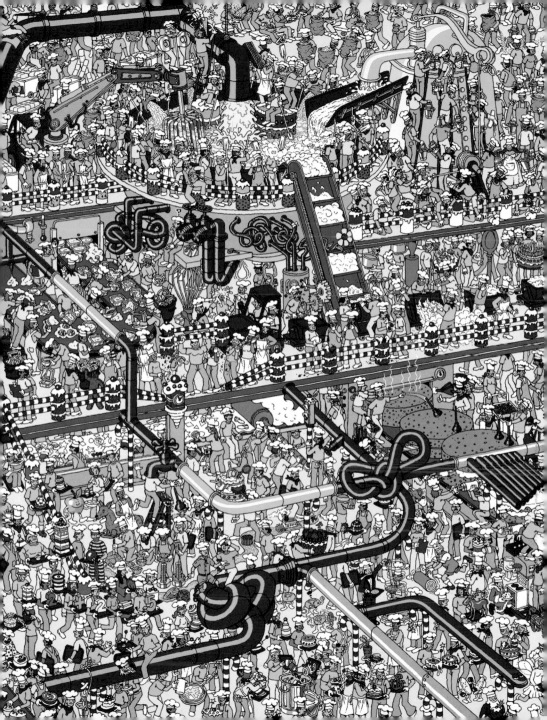

THE BATTLE OF THE BANDS

BOOM, BOOM, RAT-A-TAT-TAT! HAVE YOU EVER HEARD SUCH A BEATING OF DRUMS? ROOT-A-TOOT, TAN-TARA! OR SUCH AN EAR-SPLITTING BLAST OF TRUMPETS? A HOSTILE ARMY OF BANDSMEN IS MASSING BENEATH THE RAMPARTS OF THE GRAND CASTLE OF MUSIC. SOME ARE BEING PUSHED ALONG IN BANDSTANDS! OTHERS ARE CLIMBING MUSIC-NOTE LADDERS! BUT WHAT A STRANGE THING! THEY ARE ALL DRESSED AS ANIMALS! SEE THE ELEPHANTS, THE BEARS, THE CROCS AND THE DUCKS! AND JUST LIKE THEIR MUSIC THEY ARE WILD AND WACKY!

THE ODLAW SWAMP

THE BRAVE ARMY OF MANY HATS IS TRYING TO GET THROUGH THIS FEARFUL SWAMP. HUNDREDS OF ODLAWS AND BLACK AND YELLOW SWAMP CREATURES ARE CAUSING TROUBLE IN THE UNDERGROWTH. THE REAL ODLAW IS THE ONE CLOSEST TO HIS LOST PAIR OF BINOCULARS. CAN YOU FIND HIM, X-RAY-EYED ONES? HOW MANY DIFFERENT KINDS OF HATS CAN YOU SEE ON THE SOLDIERS' HEADS? SQUELCH! SQUELCH! I'M GLAD I'M NOT IN THEIR SHOES! ESPECIALLY AS THEIR FEET ARE IN THE MURKY MUD!

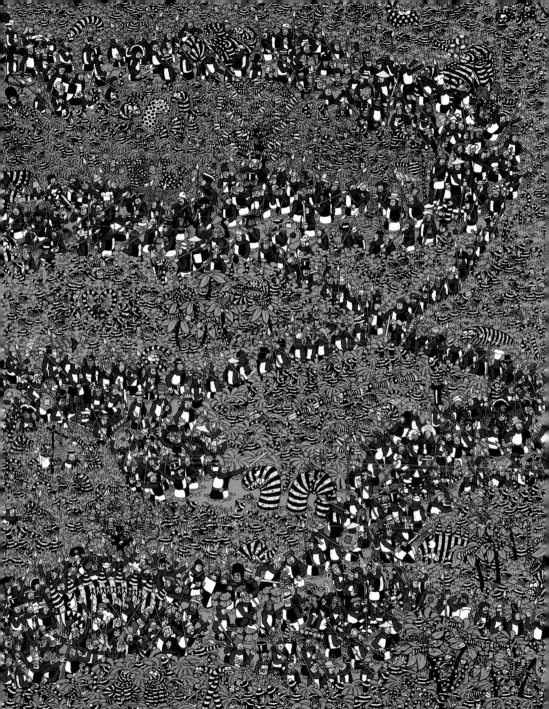

THE FANTASTIC FLOWER GARDEN

CAN YOU SEE? SNIFF THE AIR, WALLY FOLLOWERS! SMELL THE FANTASTIC SCENTS! WHAT A TREAT FOR YOUR NOSES AS WELL AS YOUR EYES!

WOW! WHAT A BRIGHT AND DAZZLING GARDEN SPECTACLE! ALL THE FLOWERS ARE IN FULL BLOOM, AND HUNDREDS OF BUSY GARDENERS ARE WATERING AND TENDING THEM. THE PETAL COSTUMES THEY ARE WEARING MAKE THEM LOOK LIKE FLOWERS THEMSELVES! VEGETABLES ARE GROWING IN THE GARDEN TOO. HOW MANY DIFFERENT KINDS

THE CORRIDORS OF TIME

TICK-TOCK, TICK-TOCK! THE HANDS OF ALL THE CLOCKS EXCEPT ONE SAY A QUARTER TO TWELVE. WHAT A DING-DONG THERE WILL BE WHEN THEY STRIKE! CAN YOU FIND THE ONLY CLOCK THAT TELLS A DIFFERENT TIME? IN THIS SCENE ARE THIRTY-SEVEN DOORS. ABOVE EACH DOOR APPEARS THE SHAPE OF THE KEY THAT WILL UNLOCK IT. CAN YOU FIND THE KEYS IN THE CROWD, BRAINY ONES, AND MATCH THEM TO THE SHAPES? OH NO! ONE DOOR HAS NO SHAPE ABOVE IT! EVEN SO YOU MUST FIND ITS KEY!

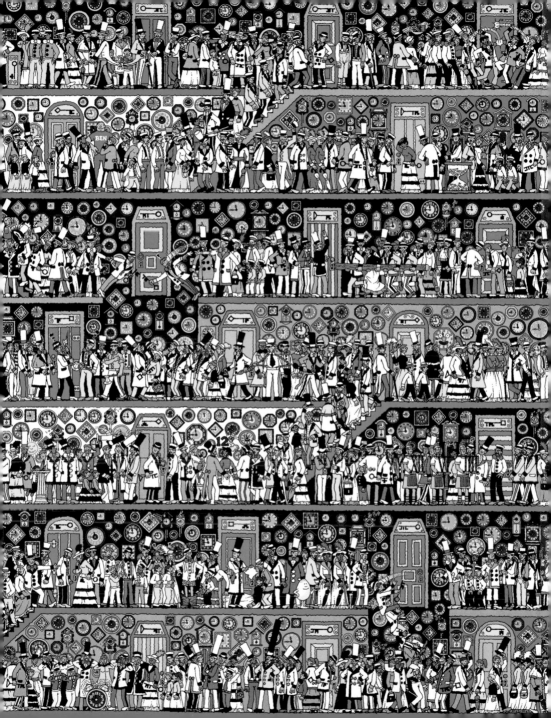

THE LAND OF WOOFS

HEY! LOOK AT ALL THESE DOGS THAT ARE DRESSED LIKE WOOF! BOW WOW WOW! IN THIS LAND, A DOG'S LIFE IS THE HIGH LIFE! THERE'S A LUXURY WOOF HOTEL WITH A BONE-SHAPED SWIMMING POOL, AND AT THE WOOF RACE TRACK LOTS OF WOOFS ARE CHASING ATTENDANTS DRESSED AS CATS, SAUSAGES AND POSTMEN! THE BOOKMARK IS ON THIS PAGE, WALLY FOLLOWERS, SO NOW YOU KNOW, THIS IS MY FAVOURITE SCENE! THIS IS THE ONLY SCENE IN THE BOOK WHERE YOU CAN SEE MORE OF THE REAL WOOF THAN JUST HIS TAIL! BUT CAN YOU FIND HIM? HE'S THE ONLY ONE WITH FIVE RED STRIPES ON HIS TAIL! HERE'S ANOTHER CHALLENGE! ELEVEN

TRAVELLERS HAVE FOLLOWED ME HERE – ONE FROM EVERY SCENE. CAN YOU SEE THEM? AND CAN YOU FIND WHERE EACH ONE JOINED ME ON MY ADVENTURES, AND SPOT ALL THEIR APPEARANCES AFTERWARDS? KEEP ON SEARCHING, WALLY FANS! HAVE A WONDERFUL, WONDERFUL TIME!

EXHIBIT 1 – ODLAW'S PICTURE PANDEMONIUM

WOW, WALLY FANS, WHAT PANDEMONIUM! HAVE YOU EVER SEEN SO MANY YELLOW-AND-BLACK STRIPES IN ONE PLACE? AMAZING! WE'RE HERE IN ODLAW'S PICTURE GALLERY AND JUST LOOK AT WHAT HIS ARTFUL ASSOCIATES HAVE BROUGHT WITH THEM – 30 PECULIAR PORTRAITS IN AN ODDITY OF FRAMES. AMAZING! THERE'S QUITE A CAST OF CHARACTERS IN THESE PAINTINGS, AND THEY ALL APPEAR AGAIN ELSEWHERE IN THE BOOK. AND PICTURE THIS – ONE OF THEM EVEN APPEARS SOMEWHERE IN THIS CRAZY CROWD! SO PATIENTLY PERUSE THE PICTURE UNTIL YOU FIND HIM. GOOD LUCK WHEREVER YOU LOOK IN YOUR HUNT FOR THE PLACES WITH THE FACES! WHAT A PICTURE!

EXHIBIT 2 –
A SPORTING LIFE

WELCOME, PICTURE HUNT PALS, TO MY SPECIAL REPORT FROM THE LAND OF SPORT. FANTASTIC! IT'S LIKE THE OLYMPICS EVERY DAY HERE, BUT WITH SO MANY ATHLETIC EVENTS ON THE MENU THERE'S NO TIME LEFT FOR ANY REST AND RELAXATION. HOWEVER, THERE'S NOTHING TOO STRENUOUS ABOUT OUR MAIN EVENT, THE GREAT PICTURE HUNT, SO KEEP YOUR EYES ON THE BALL AND HAVE YOUR POINTER FINGERS READY. ON YOUR MARKS, GET SET, GO!

EXHIBIT 5 – THE PINK PARADISE PARTY

IT'S SATURDAY NIGHT, THE TEMPERATURE IS RISING AND IT LOOKS AS IF A RASH OF MUSICAL MAYHEM AND DISCO FEVER HAS BROKEN OUT IN THIS DIZZY DANCE HALL. WOW! AMAZING! HIP HIP-HOPPERS, BODY-POPPERS, ROCK-AND-ROLLERS AND BODY-AND-SOULERS – IT'S A PACKED-OUT, PARTYGOERS' PINK PARADISE. SO GET ON DOWN, CUT YOUR GROOVE AND MAKE YOUR MOVES – IT'S TIME TO SHUFFLE YOUR FEET TO THE PICTURE HUNT BEAT!

EXHIBIT 6 – OLD FRIENDS

AH, PICTURE HUNT PALS, HOW I LOVE TO LOOK THROUGH MY SCRAPBOOKS OF MEMORIES AND SOUVENIRS. THIS PAGE IS ONE OF MY FAVOURITES: A COLLAGE CRAMMED WITH FAMILIAR FACES FROM MY EARLIER ADVENTURES. FANTASTIC! EVEN THE MOST DEDICATED OF WALLY-WATCHERS AMONG YOU WILL HAVE TROUBLE RECOGNIZING ALL OF THE OLD FRIENDS HERE – IT'S QUITE A CHALLENGE. BUT HERE'S AN EASIER TEASER THAT ANYONE CAN DO: JUST LOOK AT ALL THE CIRCLED FACES IN THIS FRAME, THEN SEE IF YOU CAN SPOT THEM IN THE SURROUNDING PICTURE.

EXHIBIT 7 – OLD FRIENDS AGAIN

IT'S ALWAYS NICE WHEN FRIENDS CAN STAY FOR
A LITTLE LONGER... I'VE CALLED THIS "OLD FRIENDS AGAIN"
BECAUSE THAT'S EXACTLY WHAT IT IS ... A FRAMED
COLLECTION OF SOME OF THE OLD FRIENDS FROM THE
PICTURE NEXT DOOR, BUT IN SILHOUETTE FORM. AND JUST
TO MAKE IT A BIT MORE INTERESTING, SOME OF THEM ARE
PICTURED UPSIDE DOWN OR SIDEWAYS. CAN YOU MATCH EACH
SILHOUETTE HERE WITH THE CORRECT OLD FRIEND IN
EXHIBIT 6? SO, ONWARDS AND UPWARDS (AND DOWNWARDS
AND SIDEWAYS), MY PICTURE HUNT PORTRAITEERS!

EXHIBIT 8 – THE MONSTER MASTERPIECE

YIKES, SPIKES AND KNOBBLY BITS, I'M LOST IN THE LAND OF THE MONSTERS. WOW! WHAT A CREATURE FEATURE! WHO'S IN CHARGE HERE, ANYWAY? THE HELMETED HUNTERS OR THEIR QUARRELSOME QUARRY? BUT DON'T BE PUT OFF BY THIS MONSTER MAYHEM, ART FANS, PLAY ON WITH THE PUZZLE, THERE ARE STILL SOME PORTRAIT SUBJECTS TO FIND. WHAT A MONSTROSITY!

EXHIBIT 9 – WALLYWORLD

WOW! WHAT A HOOPY, LOOPY WORLD WE'RE IN,
GALLERY GAZERS – NOT JUST A WORLD OF WALLIES,
BUT A WORLD OF WHITEBEARDS, WENDAS, WOOFS AND
AN ODDITY OF ODLAWS AS WELL. AMAZING! BUT LOOK
AGAIN... THERE'S ONLY ONE REAL WALLY HERE, AND THE
SAME GOES FOR MY FRIENDS, TOO. DON'T FORGET THAT
YOU CAN ONLY TELL IF WE'RE THE GENUINE ARTICLES BY
CHECKING EVERYTHING – FROM OUR GLASSES TO OUR
STRIPES. CAST YOUR EYES ACROSS THESE LINES OF
LOOKALIKES AND SEE IF YOU CAN FIND US!

EXHIBIT 10 – WALLYWORLD AGAIN

DON'T BE DAUNTED BY HAVING TO DALLY OVER THIS DIZZY DIORAMA OF DOPPELGANGERS, DEAR READERS, EVERYTHING IS NOT AS IT LOOKS. WE'RE ALL STILL HERE, BUT THIS TIME THERE ARE 20 VARIATIONS FROM THE SCENE ON THE LEFT. CAN YOU SPOT ALL THE DIFFERENCES? AND HAVE YOU FOUND THE REAL ME AND THE REAL WHITEBEARD, WENDA, WOOF AND ODLAW YET? IF YOU'RE STILL HAVING TROUBLE FINDING US, WHY NOT CHECK OUT HOW WE LOOK ON THE FIRST PAGE.

EXHIBIT 11 – PIRATE PANORAMA

SHIVER ME TIMBERS, SHIPMATES, WHAT PERFIDIOUS, PIRATE PANORAMA IS THIS? WOW! AMAZING! I'VE SAILED THE SEVEN SEAS SEARCHING FOR THESE 30 PORTRAIT PEOPLE, AND NOW THAT OUR JOURNEY IS ALMOST OVER, I JUST HOPE THE PIRATES DON'T MAKE THEM WALK THE PLANK! I'M SURE THOSE FARAWAY CASTAWAYS WOULD PREFER TO BE MAROONED ON A DESERT ISLAND THAN TO MEET THESE BARMY BUCCANEERS. ALL HANDS ON DECK!

EXHIBIT 12 – THE GREAT PORTRAIT EXHIBITION

OUR JOURNEY IS NOW OVER, PORTRAIT PERUSERS, BUT WHAT
A FITTING FINALE: A FANTASTIC EXHIBITION IN A PROPER ART
GALLERY. WOW! AMAZING! THE CROWD HERE SEEMS MUCH MORE
WELCOMING THAN ODLAW'S ODD ENSEMBLE. I'M ALSO REALLY
PLEASED THAT ALL 30 OF THE CHARACTERS WE'VE BEEN
HUNTING FOR ARE HERE AMONGST THE GALLERY GAZERS. SEE
IF YOU CAN SPOT THEM AS THEY WANDER FREELY AMONG THE
VISITORS ENJOYING THE SHOW. I HOPE YOU FOUND THEM IN THE
PREVIOUS PAGES, TOO. IF NOT, THERE'S STILL PLENTY OF TIME
TO DO SO – THE EXHIBITION NEVER CLOSES. HAPPY HUNTING!

HI WALLY-WATCHERS!

ARE YOU READY TO JOIN ME ON ANOTHER INCREDIBLE ADVENTURE WITH MORE FUN AND GAMES THAN EVER BEFORE?

I SEE SO MANY WONDERFUL THINGS ON MY TRAVELS THAT THIS TIME I AM TAKING MY NOTEPAD TO HELP ME REMEMBER THEM.

WOW! THE EXCITEMENT BEGINS RIGHT HERE – AS THE RED KNIGHTS STORM THE BLUE KNIGHTS' CASTLE WALLS. CAN YOU SPOT SOME GRINNING GARGOYLES, A GHASTLY GHOUL AND A GIANT CAKE?

THE SEARCH IS ON!

Wally

FIND WALLY, WOOF (BUT ALL YOU CAN SEE IS HIS TAIL), WENDA, WIZARD WHITEBEARD AND ODLAW IN EVERY SCENE. (DON'T BE FOOLED BY ANY CHILDREN THAT ARE DRESSED LIKE WALLY!)

FIND THE PRECIOUS THINGS THEY'VE LOST TOO: WALLY'S KEY, WOOF'S BONE, WENDA'S CAMERA, WIZARD WHITEBEARD'S SCROLL AND ODLAW'S BINOCULARS.

ONE MORE THING! CAN YOU FIND A PIECE OF PAPER THAT WALLY HAS DROPPED FROM HIS NOTEPAD IN EVERY SCENE?

THE JURASSIC GAMES

GOODNESS CRETACEOUS! WHO WILL YOU SUPPORT FROM THE SIDELINES – THE BLUE STRIPY-SAURUS TEAM OR THE PINK SPOTTY-DOCUS TEAM? WILL YOU CHEER FOR THE CRICKET, THE ROWING OR THE BASKETBALL? DON'T FORGET TO WAVE IF YOU SEE A T.REX – THEY'RE NOT IN ANY TEAM, BUT YOU WOULDN'T WANT TO GET ON THEIR WRONG SIDE!

PICTURE THIS

PHEW! LOOK AT ALL THESE FRAMED PORTRAITS. ALTHOUGH THEY MAY BE COLOURED DIFFERENTLY, SOME OF THESE ARE CHARACTERS I HAVE MET ON MY OTHER TRAVELS. THERE ARE ALSO SOME WHO APPEAR ELSEWHERE IN THIS BOOK. CAN YOU SPOT FOUR CHARACTERS THAT APPEAR TWICE IN THIS SPECTACULAR DISPLAY?

THE GREAT RETREAT

YIKES! A FEROCIOUS MAN-EATING MONSTER IS WANDERING FREE AND HE'S HUNGRY – HE'S GOBBLED 14 SOLDIERS FOR LUNCH ALREADY! I'VE DRAWN THE SHAPES OF EIGHT SOLDIERS ON THE RUN – CAN YOU MATCH THEM WITH EIGHT SOLDIERS IN THE CROWD BEFORE THE MONSTER EATS THEM FOR HIS TEA?

WHAT A DOG FIGHT!

BOW WOW WOW! TWO ARMIES ARE LOCKED IN BATTLE, ALL WITH DOG MASKS ON. ONE ARMY IS DRESSED IN BLUE, BLACK AND WHITE, AND THE OTHER IN RED, BROWN AND CREAM. CAN YOU FIND EIGHT SOLDIERS, FOUR FROM EACH SIDE, WITH SOMETHING IN ONE OF THE OTHER SIDE'S COLOURS? OH, AND WHERE IS WOOF IN THIS DOGGY SCRUM?

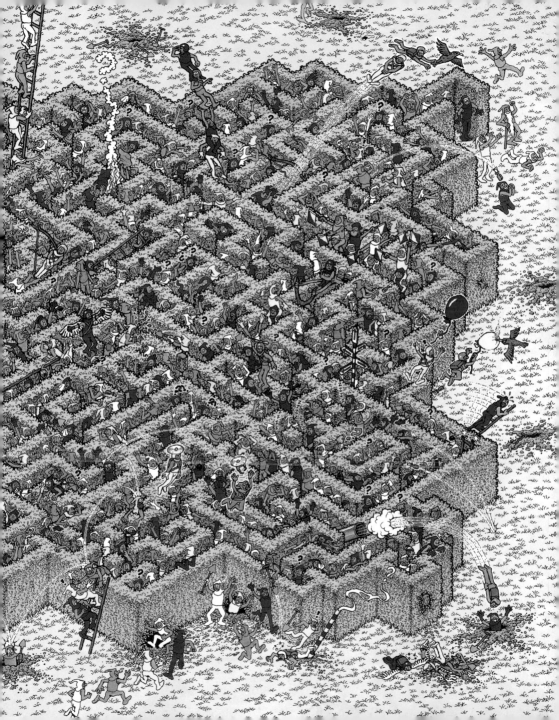

THE ENORMOUS PARTY

WOW! WHAT A BUZZ! ARE YOU
IN THE MOOD FOR A PARTY,
WALLY-WATCHERS? LOOK AT THE
BALLOONS, THE STREAMERS AND
ALL THE SMILING FACES! THE
FLAGS OF 18 COUNTRIES ARE
FLYING HERE – CAN YOU SPOT
SIX FLAGS THAT HAVE SOMETHING
WRONG WITH THEM? *

* THE ANSWERS ARE
IN PART TWO OF
THE CHECKLIST.
NO CHEATING!

This edition published 2011 by Walker Books Ltd
87 Vauxhall Walk, London SE11 5HJ

6 8 10 9 7 5

The right of Martin Handford to be identified as author/illustrator
of this work has been asserted by him in accordance with the
Copyright, Designs and Patents Act 1988

This book has been typeset in Optima and Wallyfont

Printed in China

British Library Cataloguing in Publication Data:
a catalogue record for this book is available from the British Library

ISBN 978-1-4063-3352-7

www.walker.co.uk